The Five Lost Aunts of
Harriet Bean

Also by Alexander McCall Smith

Harriet Bean and the League of Cheats
The Cowgirl Aunt of Harriet Bean

Max & Maddy and the Chocolate Money Mystery
Max & Maddy and the Bursting Balloons Mystery

Akimbo and the Elephants
Akimbo and the Lions
Akimbo and the Crocodile Man
Akimbo and the Snakes

Alexander McCall Smith

The Five Lost Aunts of Harriet Bean

Illustrated by Laura Rankin

BLOOMSBURY
CHILDREN'S
BOOKS

Published by Bloomsbury U.S.A. Children's Books
175 Fifth Avenue, New York, NY 10010
Distributed to the trade by Holtzbrinck Publishers

The Library of Congress has cataloged the hardcover edition as follows:
McCall Smith, Alexander.
The five lost aunts of Harriet Bean / by Alexander McCall Smith ;
illustrations by Laura Rankin. —1st U.S. ed.
p.   cm.
Summary: When her absent-minded inventor father suddenly remembers
that he has five sisters, nine-year-old Harriet Bean, who has never heard of
them before, determines to find her unknown aunts so that the unfinished
family portrait can be completed.
ISBN-13: 978-1-58234-975-6 • ISBN-10: 1-58234-975-4 (hardcover)
[1. Aunts—Fiction. 2. Fathers and daughters—Fiction. 3. Brothers and
sisters—Fiction.]
I. Rankin, Laura, ill. II. Title.
PZ7.M47833755Fi 2006   [Fic]—dc22   2005031523

ISBN-13: 978-1-59990-053-7 • ISBN-10: 1-59990-053-X (paperback)

Typeset by Hewer Text UK Ltd, Edinburgh
Printed in the U.S.A. by Worzalla
3 5 7 9 10 8 6 4 2

For Sophie and Anna

Contents

A Surprise Discovery

Did I ever tell you about my aunts? Well, if I didn't, that's what I'd like to tell you about now. Most people have aunts tucked away somewhere or other, and most of these aunts aren't especially interesting. It's not that I'd never want to hear about *your* aunts; it's just that there's something about my aunts that makes them very, very peculiar.

Strangely enough, I didn't even know I had any aunts until I was nine. Then, quite out of the blue, my father said to me one day:

"Your aunts would like to hear about that!"

I forget what it was that my aunts would

have liked to hear about—I was so astonished to hear that they even existed.

"Aunts?" I said in surprise. "What aunts?"

"Oh," said my father rather vaguely, as if it weren't at all important. "All those aunts of yours. You know—my sisters. All those aunts you have."

I was almost too surprised to speak. It was just like my father, though. He had always been extremely absent-minded, and he was quite capable of forgetting all about his sisters. He was a very strange man, my father, in so many ways. I won't tell you too much about him now, because it's really my aunts I want to talk about. I will tell you about his job, though, because it was so very unusual.

My father, you see, was an inventor. He invented the most extraordinary things, but unfortunately, most of them were quite useless. He was the inventor of the automatic book, for example. When you were reading an automatic book, the pages turned automatically, every few minutes. This was meant to save you the effort of turning them yourself,

but, as you can guess, different people reached the end of the page at different times. So it was always very irritating reading an automatic book, and not many of them were sold. In fact, none of his inventions was successful, and most of them came straight back from the factory with a little note saying: "Very interesting, but no, thank you" or "How remarkable—but do you think anybody really *needs* this?"

Most of the time, my father seemed to be in a bit of a daze, thinking about some strange thing he was planning to invent. Days could pass without him saying a word, and when this happened I knew that he was about to come up with an invention.

So it was not all that unusual for my father never to have mentioned his sisters, and if I did not say anything more about it, then that was all that I might have heard about the matter. But I was not going to leave it at that.

"I didn't know I had any aunts," I said, trying not to sound too annoyed. If I did then he would go out to his shed in the garden, which is what he always did when I got annoyed with him. He had an unusual invention there, which he never quite finished and which nobody was ever allowed to see.

"You didn't know you had aunts?" he said, sounding rather bemused. "How very strange!"

Well! It's hardly strange not to know you have aunts when nobody has ever said anything about them.

"Perhaps I should tell you about them," my father went on, a little doubtfully. "You are their niece, after all. Mind you, there are so many of them, I hope I don't get mixed up."

I waited for him to begin. I was dying to hear about my aunts, and yet my father seemed to forget about them almost as soon as he had mentioned them. I knew, though, that if I asked him to tell me about them at once, he would only become quiet and start to read his newspaper. So I said nothing then and waited until the next day. After he had come back from work with another rejected invention, I made him a cup of tea and a buttered scone. I knew that there was nothing he liked more than that.

"About those aunts . . . ," I began.

He glanced at me, but his eyes were fixed on the scone. "Is that for me?" he asked eagerly.

"Yes," I said. "If . . ."

My father frowned. "If what?" he asked.

"If you tell me about my aunts."

My father stared at me, and then looked again at the thickly buttered scone.

"What would you like to know about them?" he asked. "There isn't an awful lot to hear, you know."

"I want to hear everything," I said quickly. "Everything you can remember."

My father sighed.

"May I have the scone first?" he asked.

And so my father told me about my aunts, although he did not tell me the whole story in one sitting. I had to coax it out of him, and it was only after several days—and a whole plate of buttered scones—that I heard all that he had to say about my newly discovered aunts.

My father had been the only boy in the family. They lived on a small farm in those days, and there was not much money. It would have been all right if there had been just one or two children, but there were six children altogether, and that meant there were eight mouths to feed. With so many children, too, there was never enough money to buy the clothes that were needed. My father told me that he had to wear girls' shoes, handed down from his sisters. So while other boys wore proper boys' shoes, he wore red shoes with bows on them, right up until he reached the age of eight. This embarrassed him horribly. Whenever anybody came to the farm, he would quickly take his shoes off and walk around barefoot.

The children did much of the work on the farm. They did have a tractor once—my father thought it must have been one of the first tractors ever made—but it was so old that eventually it couldn't be patched up anymore. At harvest time, they used to cut the crops themselves, using scythes and sickles. And if things needed to be dragged around, they also had to do that themselves. As a result of this, he explained, most of my aunts grew up very, very strong.

Slowly, as I wrested the story out of him in dribs and drabs, I was able to build up a picture of my marvelous aunts. With a growing sense of excitement, I realized that every one of them had something rather special about her. Even to have one aunt like that would have been a treat—but to have five, well, that was very good luck indeed!

He told me first about Veronica. She was the oldest, and also the strongest. She could lift four bales of hay at once, he said, without feeling the strain. If the plow got stuck in a ditch, then they'd call Veronica. She'd walk around it for a moment or two and then, with a quick heave, she'd have it out of the ditch and back in its place.

My father told me that they were all proud

of her strength. At the agricultural show each year there was a strong man competition. All the farmhands who thought they were stronger than everybody else thought this was the highlight of the show, and they would puff and go red in the face picking up all sorts of heavy objects.

My father wanted Veronica to enter, but there was one problem. They said that the competition was for strong men, not strong women, so girls couldn't enter.

"Anyway," said the man who was in charge, "whoever heard of a strong girl?"

This sort of thing seemed very unfair to my father, and so he made a plan with Veronica. They got a hold of some boys' clothes and dressed her up in them. Then they tucked her hair up under a cap—the sort that all the farmhands wore—and there she was: a boy.

That year the strong men had to pick up pigs. There was an awfully fat pig in a pen, called Norman, and the contestants had to try to pick him up. So far, nobody had succeeded in lifting Norman. One man got two of

Norman's feet off the ground, but then Norman gave him a nip on the ankle and he dropped him.

When Veronica went forward, all the spectators had laughed.

"You're just a boy," one farmer called out. "Come back in ten years' time!"

Veronica paid no attention to all this. She paid her entrance fee and stepped into the pigpen. Then she went up to Norman and put her arms around his fat body. He really was the most enormous pig, and he must have weighed hundreds of pounds. She bent her knees and with a sudden heave, up went Norman into the air.

The pig was so surprised that he forgot to try to nip her. One moment he was enjoying a good guzzle of turnip scrapings and the next he was in the air, his feet pointing up toward the sky. He let out an awful squealing noise at first and then went absolutely silent. All the breath had been squeezed out of him by Veronica's mighty grip.

Veronica held Norman there for at least a

minute. Then she gently lowered him back onto his feet. Norman gave a gasp, followed by a grunt, and finally he lurched away to a corner. He stood there, glaring at Veronica, every rasher of his bacon quivering in fear.

Veronica was very pleased. She stepped forward to receive her prize and gave Norman a friendly pat immediately afterward. He just squealed with fright, though, and my father said that he thought Norman would remember that day for the rest of his life.

Family History

I liked the sound of Aunt Veronica. I had always hated people saying that girls are weaker than boys, and the thought of Aunt Veronica proving that this was nonsense pleased me immensely. But what about the others?

"Get me another scone," said my father, "and then I'll tell you something about your other aunts."

I buttered the largest scone I could find and set it in front of him. This seemed to put him in a very good mood, and over the next few minutes he told me all about Majolica. She was his bossy sister. She used to tell all the others what to do from the moment she got up in the morning until the time she went to bed.

"She was always shouting, *'Do this! Do that! No! Not that way!'* " said my father. "And so on.

"She had ideas about everything. If she thought somebody walked the wrong way, she'd say something about it. If she didn't like the way somebody brushed her hair, she'd tell her to change it. There was nothing she wasn't prepared to boss people over.

"Can you just imagine how bossy she was?" asked my father. "Well, I played a trick on her once, and although it didn't stop her bossing people around, it certainly kept her quiet for a day or so. It was a very good trick, and I don't have time to tell you about it now, but I will later on."

My father laughed at the memory of the mysterious trick. So far, though, he had only spoken about Veronica and Majolica, and I was eager to hear all about the others too.

"There were three others," he went on,

counting the aunts on his fingers. "Veronica was the oldest. Then, after her came the twins, Japonica and Thessalonika. I can't quite remember whether Harmonica was older than Majolica, although I do know that Japonica arrived two minutes before Thessalonika."

Harmonica was the musical one, which suited her name, of course. They had no musical instruments then, but Harmonica had the most enchanting voice anybody could imagine. She sounded like a nightingale, and visitors to the farm would stand in wonder if they heard her singing.

And she could do something else too. She was a ventriloquist, which meant that she could throw her voice. She could throw her voice into a trunk and make it sound as if there were somebody inside. She could throw it behind a curtain and make you quite positive that there was somebody standing behind it. It was a marvelous gift.

Japonica and Thessalonika could do only one thing well. They could read minds. My father supposed that it came from being twins. He said that if you have a twin, you get used to thinking about what the other person is going to do. Eventually you become able to read your twin's mind, and once you can do that, it's not so hard to read other people's minds.

They could do the most extraordinary things as a result of this ability. They could tell if somebody was lying. In fact, they could tell if somebody was going to lie even before that person opened his mouth. As my father told me about this, I thought: what a very great talent to have!

I listened to what my father had to say about my aunts. He had never talked to me about his family before and I had always assumed that there had only been him. Now I found myself with a whole set of new relatives, all of whom sounded exciting. Naturally I wanted to meet them, and so I asked him where they lived and when we could go to see them. At this, his smile disappeared.

"I have no idea where they live," he confessed. "I've got old addresses for one or two of them of course, but those are bound to be out of date. So where they are today—heaven knows!"

"But what happened?" I pressed. "You can't have lost my aunts just like that."

He nodded sadly.

"I did, I'm afraid. They're all lost, every single one of them."

I asked him how it happened and he told me the story.

"The farm we lived on really wasn't very good. The soil was thin there, and the potatoes we grew were always very hard and tiny. The animals were thin too, just as we were. The cows all showed their ribs and it was a great effort for the hens to lay any eggs.

"At last my poor parents—your grandparents—decided that we just could not go on. They called us all together and told us the bad news that they would have to sell the farm. If they got enough money from the sale, they might be able to buy a small shop in town,

and we could live off that. I liked the idea at the time. For a boy who had spent all his life on a farm, the idea of living above a shop sounded very nice.

"But things did not work out that way. When the farm was put up for sale, quite a few people came out to see it, but nobody seemed prepared to buy it for the price my father set. One or two people actually laughed when they saw how thin the soil was and how hungry the animals looked. And so your grandparents were forced to sell it for next to nothing to a man who was going to use it for no other purpose than to ride his horses over it. Our house—the house in which we had all been born and had grown up—was to have a wider door fitted and was then to be used as a stable for the horses. Oh, the shame of it!

"What was worse, though, was that we could not afford to buy the shop after all. Your grandfather was now desperate. I saw him sitting in his chair near the kitchen stove, his head in his hands, thinking about the sad fate that had befallen us. I longed to be able to help my parents, but what could I do? I couldn't get a job—I was too young for that—and nobody seemed willing to take on the girls.

"At last, when the day came to leave the farm, your grandfather broke more bad news to us.

" 'I'm very sorry,' he said. 'We are all going to have to split up. I just can't afford to keep the family together anymore.'

"It was a terrible, terrible blow, and I was so shocked by it that I almost did not hear what he then had to say. It seemed he had arranged for us to go and stay with various people all over the country. Some of the girls were to go to cousins; others were to go to live in a children's home in a city a long way off.

As the youngest, I was given the best choice. I was to live with my grandparents. Even this was a terrible fate. I did not want to leave Majolica, Veronica, and Harmonica, not to mention Thessalonika and Japonica. But I really had no choice, and that day I said good-bye to my sisters, fearing that I would never see them again. And I never have."

It seemed to me to be one of the saddest stories I had ever heard. As my father spoke, I could picture the day when they all left the farm. I had no idea what it was to have a brother or a sister—I had none—but I imagined that a brother or a sister must be the very best of friends, and to see all your brothers and sisters going off to a new home must be like losing all your best friends at once.

My father ate the last crumb of his scone and sighed. I thought that he had come to the end of his story, but he suddenly looked up and went on.

"There's something else I should tell you," he said. "When they realized that the family would have to split up, your grandparents decided that they would have a portrait of all the children painted. They got in touch with a painter who lived nearby and asked him whether he would do it. The painter was a rather temperamental man, and nobody could ever tell when he was likely to be difficult, but he agreed, and we had the first sitting.

"We dressed in our best clothes—which were all a bit threadbare, I'm afraid to say— and then we all stood in two rows, with Majolica in the middle. The painter, who was an enormous man with a handlebar mustache, fussed and fiddled with his canvas and seemed to take an awfully long time to do anything. It was difficult for us—we had to try to keep a straight face and not to move, while all the time we could hardly keep our eyes off his mustache, which went up and down whenever he moved.

"Your grandparents had hoped that the painting would be finished within three or four days, but unfortunately the painter took much longer than that. At the end of a week, as the painter was packing up and cleaning his brushes after the day's work, your grandfather explained to him that he could no longer afford to pay him.

" 'It's taken so long,' he said apologetically. 'And as we have to pay you at the end of each day, I'm afraid we will have to stop today.'

"The painter was very upset and threw his arms up and down in the air to emphasize his displeasure. But there was no alternative. He was not prepared to work without payment, and we didn't have the money to pay him any more. So he left us with an unfinished painting. All the bodies were painted, up to the shoulders. But he hadn't gotten around to even starting the heads."

I said nothing. I was trying to imagine what the painting must have been like. It must have looked very peculiar, with the six figures standing there, all with no heads.

"Would you like to see it?" my father asked.

"See what?"

"Why, the painting," he said. "I have it upstairs, you see. It's in the attic. It'll be dusty after all these years, but it's there all right."

The Search Begins

Now this was exciting news indeed! Together with my father I made my way up into the attic, a dark and dusty place full of all sorts of bits and pieces that had been stored away over the years. In spite of the confusion, though, my father seemed to know exactly where to look. Muttering to himself, he gave a tug at a large square object and there, covered, as he had warned, with a thick layer of dust, was the painting.

We took it downstairs and rubbed it down with a cloth. Clouds of dust flew up and slowly the picture on the canvas began to show itself. I peered at it as the figures emerged. Yes! There they were, in two rows, surrounding the youthful figure of my father, my aunts! (Or, rather, parts of my aunts—up as far as their necks.)

I polished away at the painting until it was as clean as I could get it.

"Yes," said my father. "There we are. And that's one of the barns in the background. That's me with the torn trousers. And that's Veronica—can you see the strong arms? And that's Thessalonika. She always wore that pink dress on Sundays although it had become very tattered."

It made me sad to look at the picture. If only there had been enough money to pay the painter to finish it, then there would at least have been a good record of the family. There were the photographs, of course, but you can't really put photographs on your wall, and when they're tucked away in an album they're rather out of mind.

"I wish it had been finished," I said. "If only the painter had worked faster."

My father nodded. "Now it will never be finished," he mused. "And it's no good as it is, with blanks where the heads should be."

It was as he spoke that an idea occurred to me. Unfinished paintings *can* be finished, even if it's years later. Perhaps I could trace my aunts. Perhaps I could get them all together again and we could have the painting finished at last. Although my grandfather was no longer alive, it would be a marvelous thing to finish off the one thing that he had wanted so much and that had not worked out for him.

I turned to my father.

"Couldn't we get the painting finished?" I asked. "If we found my aunts again and got them together . . ."

My father thought for a moment. He looked doubtful.

"I've lost touch," he said. "I've got one or two addresses somewhere, but it's all so long ago."

I was determined to persevere.

"Please, let's try," I said. "Please, let's see if we can do it."

"I'll think about it," my father said. "Maybe."

Over the next few days, I thought about little else. My father, though, appeared to forget about it all and seemed rather surprised when I asked him for the addresses he had told me about.

"I want to write to my aunts," I said to him. "Could you give me those addresses you had?"

He looked at me vaguely. "Aunts? Oh yes, of course, all those aunts." He frowned. "I don't think the addresses will be any use. They're from about ten years ago."

I insisted that I still wanted to try, and, grumbling under his breath about being disturbed, he went off to search in a drawer of his desk. His desk was always overflowing with bits of paper, and I was astonished that he ever managed to find anything there.

At last he came back with a scrap of paper.

"This is the only one I can find," he said. "I don't know what happened to the others."

I took the piece of paper with trembling hands. The name Veronica was written at the top, and underneath there was the number of a house and a street in a town with a name I had never heard before. I fetched my diary and carefully transferred the information to a page at the back. The search had begun.

I did not write a long letter to Aunt Veronica. All I did was introduce myself and tell her that the only reason why I had not written before was that my father had never told me of her existence.

"You must have thought me very rude," I wrote, "not even to send you a Christmas card. But it really is my father's fault. Now I am writing to make up for it all."

I sent the letter, dropping it into the mailbox with a silent wish that it would find its destination. Then, for the next ten days, I eagerly awaited the arrival of the mailman.

"Anything for me?" I asked as he made his way up the garden path.

The answer was always the same.

"Nothing today. Sorry."

Nothing. Nothing. Nothing. And then . . .

When the mailman handed me the letter, I could hardly believe that it had really come. I examined the postmark and caught my breath as I saw that it was from the very town I had written. It was a letter from Aunt Veronica—that was all it could be.

There was a single page inside. "Dear Harriet Bean," I read. "I opened the letter that you sent to your aunt because I now live in that house and it was delivered to me. If I knew where to send it, I could have forwarded it on to her unopened. But I'm afraid that I have no idea where she is. She went away from here years ago and did not leave a new address. All I can say is that I believe that she worked in a circus. This meant that she was away from home most of the time and never had the time to make many friends. So nobody knows where she is anymore. I'm very sorry, and I do hope that you find her."

I put the letter down and closed my eyes.

I was bitterly disappointed, but I knew that I was not going to give up. At least I now had a clue. Aunt Veronica worked in a circus. There were probably quite a number of circuses, and I might not find the right one, but I was sure to discover somebody in the circus world who had met her or who would know something about her.

I had not been told what she did in the circus, though, and that could make my search more difficult. Did she sell tickets in the box office? Did she work with horses, or even lions? Or was she one of those people who swing on the high trapeze? All of these were possible.

From then on, I studied the newspaper every day to see if there were any circuses performing nearby. There were all sorts of other events—concerts, races, motorcycle shows—but nothing about a circus. Then, at last, just when I was beginning to think that circuses had disappeared altogether, my eye fell on a small notice at the bottom of the page.

"Circus Romano," it said simply. "A great treat for all! Don't miss it!" This was followed by the dates and places, and one of the places was not far away.

I took the advertisement and showed it to my father.

"Please take me to the circus," I begged. "I've never been to one before."

My father looked at the notice and wrinkled up his nose.

"Nasty, noisy things," he said. "I'm sure you wouldn't enjoy yourself."

"But I would," I protested. "I really want to go."

He could tell that I was very eager to do this, and because, in spite of all his faults (and he has a lot of them), he's really very kind inside, he said that we could go. I was delighted. This was my first chance of finding Aunt Veronica, and I had a feeling that I was going to be lucky the first time.

A Trip to the Circus

The days of waiting for the Circus Romano dragged painfully. I began to have doubts about what would happen when I met Aunt Veronica. What would I say to her?

"How do you do? You're my aunt." That sounded rather abrupt. Perhaps I should say, "I'm sorry to bother you, but I think I'm your niece."

And what would her reply be? Would she be pleased, or would she be annoyed? Perhaps she wouldn't want a niece. Perhaps she'd think that I wanted something from her.

By the time we left for the circus, I felt very anxious indeed and the sight of the great tent and its glare of lights did nothing to calm my fears. I had made no plan about what to do at the circus, although I hoped that I would have the chance to ask some of the performers after the show whether they knew anything of Aunt Veronica.

We took our seats by the ringside. My father had bought good tickets—the best available, in fact—and so we were seated right at the very edge of the ring. He was still not at all interested in the whole thing, and he looked around with disapproval.

"Look at those trapezes," he said, pointing to the silver swings suspended from the very top of the tent. "What a ridiculous place to put them. Why don't they put them closer to the ground so we can all see what's happening?"

I tried to explain to him that what made trapezes so exciting was the fact that they were so high, but he seemed to take no interest. So I sat back and waited for the show to begin.

With a fanfare from the circus band the first act began. This was horses—marvelous, jet-black animals bedecked in glittering harnesses, plumes rising proudly above their heads. As they cantered around the ring, a great cheer rose from the crowd.

The horses were followed by clowns. They fell down, squirted each other with water, and played the trombone as they tripped each other up. The audience loved them, or rather, *most* of the audience loved them. My father just sat and stared at them, shaking his head in disbelief.

"Silly people," he muttered. "I don't see what's so funny about having a red nose and tripping over your feet."

Then, when the clowns had left, a circle of stout iron bars was set up around the ring and a man in a red coat and top hat strutted proudly to the center. This was the lion tamer, and at the crack of his whip five great lions bounded in through a tunnel. Everyone gasped as the lions sprang onto stools and bared their vicious-looking teeth at the trainer. Everyone, that is, except my father. He took out a newspaper he had tucked into his jacket pocket, unfolded it, and began to read.

My father was still reading when the lions had disappeared and their cage had been dismantled. He was still buried in his newspaper when the next act started, and so he did not see the strong woman march into the ring, nor see her flex her bulging muscles for the admiration of the crowd. I saw her, though, and knew in my heart that this was my Aunt Veronica. I had found her.

"Ladies and gentlemen!" cried the ringmaster. "This strong lady, the strongest lady in the country, will now demonstrate her mighty strength. She will begin by tearing up three telephone directories all stuck together!"

"Impossible!" called a voice from the back of the tent, but Aunt Veronica did not bat an eyelid. She took the directories from the ringmaster, held them before her, and then, with one great rip, tore them in two.

There was a burst of applause and one or

two jeers directed against the man who had shouted out that it was impossible. There was applause too, for her next feat, which was to bend a thick iron bar until its ends touched one another, and for the feat after that, in which she picked up a piece of railway line with her teeth.

"Now," said the ringmaster, "the strong lady will take on the circus elephant in a tug-of-war!"

Laughter and clapping greeted the plodding arrival in the ring of the circus elephant. Coolly and calmly, Aunt Veronica tied one end of a thick rope to the elephant's trunk and then braced herself against the other end. Then the two of them tugged away, but try as it might, the elephant could not move Aunt Veronica.

The applause almost brought the tent down around our ears. Aunt Veronica bowed, raised her hands in the air, and then led the elephant to the side of the ring to stand there while she performed her final and most difficult feat.

I watched in fascination as Aunt Veronica lay down on the ground. Then, on top of her stomach, three circus assistants laid heavy iron weights, each the size of a football. They were burying my aunt in iron weights! Only one of these weights would have crushed the breath out of an ordinary person, and Aunt Veronica now had at least fifteen piled on top of her.

Suddenly my father lowered his newspaper. I think it was the silence that made him wonder what was going on. He looked into the ring, opened his eyes wide with surprise at the strange sight of the weighted-down strong lady, and then gave a sudden jolt.

"Veronica!"

Aunt Veronica heard my father's exclamation and turned to look in his direction. Their eyes met, and I think that she recognized him immediately.

My father was now on his feet.

"Veronica!" he called out again. "Surely it can't be you?"

"Harold!" Aunt Veronica called out from under her weights. "Is it really you, Harold?"

Without further ado, my father leapt from his seat and vaulted into the ring.

"No," shouted the ringmaster from the other side. "Keep out, sir!"

My father ignored the ringmaster's cry and began to run across the ring to his long-lost sister. I watched, fascinated—proud to have found my aunt, but embarrassed by my father's behavior. Why could he not have waited until the end of the act? There would have been plenty of time for reunions then.

The ringmaster called out another warning, but it was too late. The elephant had been disturbed by my father's sudden arrival in the ring and had lumbered forward to meet him. Now, before my father could do anything about it, the elephant had grabbed him with his trunk and wound it around him.

"My father!" I cried. "He's going to be squeezed to pieces!"

I watched in horror as my father turned a strange purple color. I was convinced that this

was the end, and I was powerless to do anything about it.

When Aunt Veronica saw what was happening, she lost no time in throwing off the iron weights. With a great shrug and *hurrumph* she pushed the weights away and staggered to her feet. Then, with one or two bounds, she dashed across to the elephant.

The elephant had now unwound part of my father and had laid him on the ground. I thought that it was going to release him, but I soon realized that it had other plans. Slowly, but very deliberately, the elephant was beginning to sit on my father!

I closed my eyes in horror. Only a miracle could save him now . . . or Aunt Veronica. When I opened my eyes again, she was in between my father and the elephant, pushing the elephant up and away. The elephant looked very annoyed and gave a bellow of anger. Then, realizing that it had met its match, it ambled away and looked resentfully at my aunt.

As if it were one person, the crowd rose to its feet in applause.

"Bravo!" they shouted. "Well done!"

My father, looking a bit shaken, but otherwise none the worse for his experience, was led back to his seat by Aunt Veronica.

"You must be my niece," she said, smiling at me in a very friendly way. "Just look after your father for the rest of the show and then we'll meet in my trailer when it's all over."

She smiled again and then, with applause still thundering to the very top of the tent, she bounded out of the ring and was gone.

Aunt Veronica's Trailer

The moment the show came to an end, I led my father out of the tent. He was eager to get out quickly, as he was well aware that everybody was looking at him.

"There's the man who was nearly sat on by the elephant!" people said, pointing to my father.

Once outside, we went straight to the corner of the field where the trailers were parked. There were at least twenty of them—brightly colored vehicles with curtains in the windows and small chimneys poking out through the top of their roofs.

I asked a boy standing outside the door of

one of the trailers to show me which one belonged to Aunt Veronica. He pointed to a small trailer near the edge of the field.

When I knocked, Aunt Veronica opened the door immediately and stood before us, her arms wide open in a gesture of welcome. She gave my father a hug, then turned her attention to me.

"I'm so glad you've come," she said enthusiastically. "I always wanted a niece, and now, presto, I find that I've had one all along!"

We went into the trailer and sat down at a table, which had just been laid for us. It was not a very large trailer, but it seemed very comfortable, with everything tidily stacked in its place. Aunt Veronica put a teakettle on a small gas stove in one corner and then took a large cake out of a cake tin.

Then, over a cup of steaming tea and a large slice of delicious fruitcake, we talked. My father had a lot to tell her, and she had a lot to tell him. Not all that much had happened in my life, so I just sat and listened to the two of them.

Finally, Aunt Veronica finished talking about herself and leaned back in her chair.

"What about the others?" she asked. "Have you heard from them?"

"The others?" asked my father.

"Majolica and Harmonica," said Aunt Veronica. "And Japonica and Thessalonika."

My father shook his head. "I'm afraid I don't know where they are." He paused. "Do you?"

Aunt Veronica sighed. "Only one of them," she said. "Harmonica. I'm sure I know where she is."

This was the signal for me to interrupt. "Oh, please, tell me," I said. "I want to find them—all of them."

Aunt Veronica looked at me thoughtfully. "Do you really want to find your aunts?" she said. "You're not just saying that?"

"No," I protested. "I mean, yes. I do want to find them." I did not want to tell her about the painting, at least not yet.

She thought for a bit longer. Then,

winking at me in a way which said, "I have a good idea," she came up with her suggestion.

"Harold," she said, turning to my father, "I think that you should leave Harriet with me for a few days. I'd like to find these sisters of mine myself, and I could do with a bit of help. I'm due a bit of vacation from the circus and now's as good a time to take it as any."

My father looked at me vaguely. "Would you like that?" he asked.

I could hardly contain my excitement. To stay with Aunt Veronica, in her trailer, and go in search of the other aunts sounded like the most magnificent idea.

"Of course I'd like that," I said. "There's nothing I'd like better."

We waved good-bye to my father as he made his way out of the circus field. Then, closing the door behind us, Aunt Veronica showed me which bunk I could have. She pointed out a cupboard where I could keep my shoes and in another cupboard she found me a spare toothbrush and soap dish.

"I'll get you some more clothes tomorrow," she said. "One of the trapeze artists has a daughter just your size. She'll lend us some clothes while you're with me. Circus people always share."

I looked around the trailer. It seemed to me the ideal place to live and travel. It had everything, or so I thought, until I noticed something strange. All the other trailers in the field were motorized, which meant that they had engines to drive them along. As far as I could make out, there was no space in this trailer for an engine. There was a driver's seat, steering wheel, and something that looked like a brake. But that was all.

Aunt Veronica noticed me looking around and she must have guessed what was going through my mind.

"Come," she said to me. "Let me show you a secret."

She led me to the front of the trailer and opened a trapdoor immediately in front of the driver's seat.

"There," she said. "That's how it works."

I looked down. There, just below the level of the floor, was a large set of pedals, exactly like the pedals of a bicycle. I gasped with surprise.

"Do you mean to say this trailer is pedal-powered?" I asked disbelievingly.

"Yes," said Aunt Veronica. "I find that it keeps my leg muscles in good shape, although sometimes it's rather hard going on hills."

I was completely astounded. Was there no end to the feats of strength of this utterly amazing aunt?

We got into our bunks, and Aunt Veronica turned the light out.

"Goodnight, Harriet," she said into the darkness. "And thank you for finding me."

I lay tucked warmly in my bunk, filled with happiness. For a while I listened to the sounds of the circus outside—the stamping of the horses' feet in their pen as they settled for the night, the growl of a lion as it moved in its sleep. Then I drifted off to sleep myself, to dream that I was as strong as Aunt Veronica and could do everything, or almost everything, that she could do.

The next morning we sat and ate our breakfast on the steps of the trailer. The circus people got up very early and were bustling around, attending to the one-hundred-and-one morning tasks of a circus. From my seat on the steps, I watched the lion tamer, no longer wearing his splendid red lion-taming outfit but clad in a pair of scruffy pajamas. He took a large pail of meat to the edge of the lions' cage and tossed their breakfast in to them.

Aunt Veronica ate a very large breakfast.

"I need it to keep my strength up," she explained, as she dug into her fourteen-egg omelette. Then, when the eggs were finished, she ate seven or eight sausages, and followed them up with ten pieces of toast.

"We will set off this morning," she said, wiping her lips on a red-checked napkin she had spread on her lap. "With any luck, we shall meet up with your Aunt Harmonica tonight."

"But where is she?" I asked. "Do you know exactly where to find her?"

Aunt Veronica nodded. "I haven't seen her for a year or two," she said. "But I know where she works. There's an opera house not all that far away. She has a job there."

We got up and washed the breakfast dishes and stacked them away. Then Aunt Veronica left for a few minutes to tell the ringmaster that she was taking a vacation. I made my bunk in the trailer and swept the floor.

When Aunt Veronica came back, I watched in fascination as she settled herself in the driver's seat of the trailer and opened the trapdoor that exposed the pedals.

"You sit in the back," she said. "You'll get a good view from the window."

And with that, she lowered her feet through the trapdoor, took a deep breath, and began to pedal.

You would never have thought it possible. There we were in a trailer—not a big one, but a trailer nonetheless—and Aunt Veronica was making it move purely through her own effort. As we drove through the field, faces appeared at the windows of the other trailers. Word spreads quickly in the circus, and the other circus people already knew about Aunt Veronica's vacation.

"Good luck!" somebody shouted. "Come back soon!"

Aunt Veronica tooted the trailer's horn, a rubber bulb attached to a brass tube, and I waved from my window. Then we were out on the open road and the trailer began to pick up speed.

We had traveled for at least an hour before Aunt Veronica began to feel tired. During this time, we had moved at about the speed of a fast bicycle, which is not all that slow. We had overtaken one or two cars as well, and I had watched the expressions of surprise on the faces of the drivers as the trailer swept silently past them. I could imagine them saying to themselves, "I didn't hear that behind me! What an amazingly quiet engine that trailer must have."

As we neared a small roadside filling station, Aunt Veronica signaled that she was going to turn in. We stopped at the side of the station and went in to buy a bottle of lemonade and a large bar of chocolate for Aunt Veronica. After we had made our purchases, Aunt Veronica turned to me, winked, and spoke to the mechanic who ran the station.

"I think I have engine trouble in my trailer," she said. "Could you take a look at it?"

The mechanic nodded, put on his greasy overalls, and walked with us back to the trailer. First he went to the front of the trailer, looked at it, and then went to the back. He opened the back door, looked at the floor, and scratched his head. Then he got down on his hands and knees and peered underneath.

"Excuse me," he said after a while. "I can't seem to find the engine. Do you know where it is?"

Aunt Veronica pretended to look puzzled. "It must be there somewhere," she said. "But I'm afraid I don't know where."

The mechanic was now looking very mystified. He crouched down again and crawled underneath.

"It's not here," he called out. "There's . . . there's absolutely nothing!"

He scrambled out and looked at Aunt Veronica, his eyes wide with astonishment.

"Where do you put the gas in?" he demanded. "Maybe we can work it out from there."

"Gas?" said Aunt Veronica, as if the word meant nothing to her. "Well, I don't think I ever buy gas. Or at least I can't actually remember ever putting any gas in."

The mechanic's jaw dropped. "You mean . . . ," he began to say. "You mean to say that you *never* put gas in?"

Aunt Veronica shook her head.

"In that case," said the mechanic, "how did you get here? You tell me that!"

Aunt Veronica shrugged her shoulders.

"I get in and turn the engine on, and just drive," she answered. "Look, I'll show you."

We both got back into the trailer and

closed the door behind us. Trying not to laugh, I took up my place at the window while Aunt Veronica sat in the driver's seat. Then, while the bemused mechanic stood back and watched, Aunt Veronica put her feet on the pedals and slowly we moved off.

"You see," she called from her seat. "It works!"

"Good-bye!" I cried as we moved off.

The mechanic stood rooted to the spot. His face was a picture of puzzlement, and he looked just as if he had seen a flying saucer.

"He'll never forget today," joked Aunt Veronica. "He'll tell all his friends about it. And do you know, I'm afraid that not one of them will ever believe him!"

The Strangest Incident in the History of Opera

The opera house stood on the top of a hill, on the outskirts of town. It was a beautiful building, as an opera house should be, with a sweep of stone steps leading up to the doors and a high roof of shining copper. We parked the trailer at the back and made our way to the stage door.

"Now, ladies," said an attendant in a blue and gold uniform, barring our way. "This door is only for the singers and musicians."

Aunt Veronica explained to him that we wished to see one of the singers.

"She's my sister," she went on. "And this is her niece."

At the mention of Aunt Harmonica's name, the attendant smiled.

"Well, well!" he said. "Now that you mention it, I can see the resemblance, although I must say you seem a bit . . . a bit more . . ."

"Muscular?" interrupted Aunt Veronica.

The attendant blushed. "Yes," he said. "You see, she's so much more . . . so much more . . ."

"Large?" suggested Aunt Veronica.

The attendant blushed even further.

"Er, yes," he said feebly. "I suppose that's true."

He motioned us to follow him and we began down a dark corridor that seemed to bore into the very heart of the opera house. It was a lovely corridor, with doors opening off into brightly lit dressing rooms and dark, cluttered storerooms. At last the attendant pointed to a half-open door and nodded his head.

"That's where she'll be," he said. "But make sure you don't distract her too much. The performance starts in less than fifteen minutes."

. . .

"You go in first," whispered Aunt Veronica. "Let's give her a surprise."

I was reluctant to do this, but I was given a good shove by Aunt Veronica and soon found myself standing in a dressing room. There were several glittery dresses hanging on a wardrobe door and a bright mirror surrounded by bulbs. On a stool before the mirror, a comfortable-looking woman was applying lipstick to her fleshy red lips. I cleared my throat to attract her attention.

I think I must have given her a bit of a fright, as she spun around sharply and looked at me with complete surprise.

"What do you want?" she asked. Then, tossing the lipstick onto the dressing table, she asked me who I was.

I drew in my breath to give my answer, but suddenly she stopped.

"Don't tell me," she said, rising to her feet to peer more closely at me. "There's something very familiar about your face."

She bent down and stared into my face from a distance of no more than a few inches.

Then she drew back and narrowed her eyes. "You don't have a father called Harold, do you?" she asked.

It was at this point that Aunt Veronica popped her head round the door.

"Yes, she does," she said.

When she saw Aunt Veronica, Aunt Harmonica burst out with a peal of triumphant laughter.

"I knew it!" she crowed. "I could tell that she was my niece."

Then she hugged me, pressing me against her vast shape, making me feel as if I had been swallowed by a giant pudding. I struggled for breath and eventually broke away from her embrace. Aunt Harmonica was crying with emotion.

"Oh, what a marvelous day this is turning out to be!" she crooned. "First, the chance to sing a lovely part tonight, and then the visit from you!"

She sat down, weeping with excitement and emotion. Aunt Veronica helped her dry her eyes and then assisted her to squeeze into her dress. As Aunt Harmonica dressed, she told us about her job.

"I would have liked to be the leading lady in operas," she said wistfully. "And I could sing well enough for that, couldn't I, Veronica?"

Aunt Veronica nodded her agreement and Aunt Harmonica went on.

"But when they discovered I could throw my voice, they wanted me to do something else. They gave me a job as an understudy."

She paused, looking at me. "You may not know what an understudy is, Harriet. An understudy is the person who's ready to take over if a singer gets a sore throat and can't sing. The show has to go on, as you know, and it's the understudy who steps in and sings. Anyway, they realized that an understudy who could throw her voice was one in a million. This meant that the first singer could go on the stage as usual and just pretend to sing. She'd just open her mouth, though, and I would throw my voice from the wings. The singers loved this. They got all the cheers and flowers at the end, while I did all the work!"

I felt sorry for Aunt Harmonica as she told me her story. It must have been terrible to have to watch others getting all the praise for her singing.

She dabbed a handkerchief at the corner of her eyes.

"Still," she went on, "there's no point in complaining about our lot in life. It's my job and . . . good heavens! Look at the time! I'm going to have to sing in five minutes. The leading lady has quite lost her voice and I'm to do her singing. So, come along, you can stand beside me and see how it's done."

I was thrilled to be able to stand beside Aunt Harmonica and watch the preparation on the stage. Everybody was in position now, including the opera star who had lost her voice. Down in the orchestra pit, the orchestra was playing the overture, and on the other side of the stage they were preparing to raise the curtain. Aunt Harmonica looked at me, smiled, and reached into her bag for a throat lozenge.

"I always suck one of these quickly before

I sing," she whispered. "It lubricates my vocal cords."

The curtain began to rise and the chorus of opera singers standing at the back of the stage burst into song. Aunt Harmonica was following what was going on very carefully, ready to begin her part when her cue came.

Suddenly I noticed that there was something wrong with Aunt Harmonica. She had raised her hands to her throat and was clutching at it frantically. Her face was beginning to turn purple—more or less the color my father had turned when the elephant had coiled its trunk around him.

I realized almost immediately what had happened. The throat lozenge which Aunt Harmonica had been sucking must have stuck in her throat and now she was not only breathless but voiceless. I turned to Aunt Veronica and tugged at her arm.

"Oh my goodness!" muttered Aunt Veronica, slapping her sister on the back. "There's something stuck in her throat."

She gave her a few more slaps on the back,

but it did not seem to do any good. Aunt Veronica then did something which seemed very strange at the time but which was obviously the right thing to do. Reaching down, she picked Aunt Harmonica up by her legs and held her upside down. There was a strange wheezing sound and then a gasp. The lozenge had moved.

Aunt Veronica placed Aunt Harmonica back on her feet, but unfortunately, this made the lozenge lodge again. Quickly she turned her upside down again, and the lozenge moved again.

"Keep me like this," Aunt Harmonica said. "It's the only way I'm going to be able to sing."

And sing she did, all the time being held upside down by Aunt Veronica. It was a very strange thing to see—an aunt being held in such an unusual position, all the while throwing her voice over the stage to where the leading lady was merely opening her mouth and pretending to sing. I am sure it was the very strangest incident in the whole history of opera.

But there was something even stranger. If you have ever heard anybody sing upside down (and you probably haven't), then you might realize that the words come out . . . upside down! Yes! And this is exactly what happened. Although Aunt Harmonica's voice sounded very tuneful, the song she was singing was definitely upside down.

By craning my neck a little, I could just see the audience past the edge of the curtain. At first they appeared not to notice anything, but after a few moments I saw that some of them were looking a little bit puzzled. Then one or two of them began to twist their heads around, and soon most people were doing this. By getting their heads just about as close as they could to being upside down, they heard the words perfectly. It was all very strange indeed.

At the end of the act, the curtain came down and Aunt Veronica was able to carry the upside down Aunt Harmonica back to her dressing room. There, with the aid of a glass of water, which Aunt Harmonica managed to drink, the lozenge was dislodged from its place and Aunt Harmonica was able to stand on her feet again, the right way up.

"What a terrible thing to happen," she gasped. "But what a stroke of luck that you were there to deal with it, Veronica."

After the opera was finished, and the singer who hadn't sung had gone out to receive her flowers from an admiring audience, Aunt Harmonica came with us to the trailer. Aunt Veronica put on the teakettle and brewed a pot of tea while I told my newfound aunt all about my life.

"I'm so glad you came to see me," Aunt Harmonica said. "I know that you have no shortage of aunts, but you're the only niece I have."

I told her that so far I had only found two aunts out of the five and asked her whether she could help to discover the rest.

"I wish I could," she said. "But I haven't seen any of them for years and years. Veronica's the only one I've come across."

I felt a wave of disappointment overcome me. I had very much hoped that Aunt Harmonica would have some information about the others, but it looked as if she knew as little as my father did.

She scratched her head.

"Now wait," she said. "Something's coming back to me at last. Yes, I think I may be able to help."

She turned to Aunt Veronica.

"Is there room for me in this trailer?" she asked, looking about her as she spoke.

Aunt Veronica glanced at the well-padded form of her sister and gulped.

"I'm sure there is," she said.

"In that case," said Aunt Harmonica, "I think I might be able to track down the others. Why don't I stay here tonight, and we will all leave together first thing in the morning."

Aunt Veronica prepared a bunk for Aunt Harmonica, and although it was a very tight squeeze, eventually Aunt Harmonica managed to settle under her blankets and the light was put out.

I closed my eyes and waited for sleep to overcome me. Suddenly, from under my bunk, I heard a small voice cry out, "Help! I'm trapped!"

I jumped out, switched on a light, and looked under the bunk. There was nothing there.

"What on earth are you doing?" asked Aunt Harmonica.

"There was somebody under my bunk," I said. "I heard a voice."

"I'm sure it was just your imagination," said Aunt Veronica sleepily.

"But I heard it!" I protested. "I wasn't dreaming."

Then I looked at Aunt Harmonica and noticed that she was smiling. At once I realized what had happened. That's exactly the sort of thing one must expect from a ventriloquist aunt.

I laughed, switched off the light, and got back into my bunk.

"Good night!" said a small voice in the darkness. It came from under my pillow, but I ignored it and soon there was silence.

Calling All Children!

I was fairly pleased with myself for having found two aunts so far, but I was certainly not prepared to leave it at that. The next morning, as the three of us sat in a small café and ate delicious apricot rolls for our breakfast, we discussed how we would find the others.

"I have no idea what happened to Thessalonika and Japonica," said Aunt Harmonica.

"Nor do I," said Aunt Veronica rather sadly.

"But I think I might know what Majolica did," went on Aunt Harmonica. "Once, many years ago, I received a birthday card from her. I'm not sure how she found my address, but it was definitely from her. And on this card she told me that she had become a teacher. That's all she said. And she forgot to put her address on it."

"That's not much of a clue," reflected Aunt Veronica. "There are teachers all over the place. Every town has its teachers."

"I know that," said Aunt Harmonica, sounding rather irritated, but cheering up as she helped herself to another apricot roll. "But remember that there was something rather special about Majolica."

"Her bossiness?" I asked, remembering what my father had told me.

My two aunts laughed.

"Exactly," said Aunt Harmonica. "And I think that we might just be able to use that to lead us to her!"

I was puzzled by this, but as Aunt Harmonica explained her scheme, I began to understand how it might work. It was an ingenious plan, and it might be a complete failure, but it was better than nothing.

We needed a good place for the trailer, as Aunt Harmonica's plan would take at least a week to put into effect. So we found a farmer who was happy to let us camp on his land, and we parked in a field by the side of a river.

It was a beautiful spot. In the evenings, as we waited for our dinner to be ready, we would sit and watch the cows amble back from their pasture. Then, as the shadows grew longer, Aunt Veronica would make a fire in a small ring of stones, and we would barbecue the juicy trout that we had caught in the river that afternoon.

In the mornings, while the two aunts talked, I would wander the fields and watch the rabbits darting in and out of their burrows. I would also pick wildflowers, which I brought back and arranged in vases in the trailer, or, sometimes, if I was feeling energetic, I would help the farmer's wife weed her vegetable patch and feed her ducks.

But while all this was going on, our plan to find Aunt Majolica was in full swing, and it's time for you to hear about it.

That first morning when Aunt Harmonica had explained her idea, we went to the office of the local newspaper and put in an advertisement. At the same time, Aunt Veronica paid for advertisements to be placed in ten other newspapers in nearby towns. Each of them said the same thing:

CALLING ALL CHILDREN!

Is there a bossy teacher in your school? And we don't mean just an ordinarily bossy teacher, we mean a teacher who is really, really bossy! If there is, then write to us and tell us about her. (We only want to hear about the bossy lady teachers, I'm afraid.) The person who has the bossiest teacher will win an interesting prize!

Now, five days later, we were beginning to wonder when we would hear. Aunt

Harmonica had told the post office where we were staying, and at last, at the end of the fifth day, a small van drew up at the edge of the field and a man called us over.

"I've got ten sacks of letters for you," he said, looking quite hot and bothered about it. "It's going to take me ages to carry them across to your trailer."

Aunt Veronica shook her head.

"Give them to me," she said firmly. "I'll do it."

The mailman laughed.

"I'm sorry, ma'am," he said. "They're very heavy. I'll have to carry them."

Aunt Veronica was used to this sort of thing, and so she wasted no time arguing. Going to the back of the van, she reached in for the sacks and was soon carrying them all under one arm. The man stood in amazement, his mouth wide open.

"That's amazing," he said. "Those sacks weigh a ton. You should be in a circus if you can do things like that."

"She is," I said.

Then, thanking him for delivering the letters, we went back to the trailer and began the immense task of sorting them out.

The letters came from all over the place. There was no alternative but to open each one and read what it had to say. Then we could put them into one of three piles. One pile was called "Definitely not Majolica." Another pile was called "Might just be Majolica." And the third pile, the important pile, we called "Sounds just like Majolica!"

My task was to open the letters. Then I handed them on to Aunt Veronica or Aunt Harmonica, who would skim through them and decide which pile to put them in. Some of the letters were very funny, and we all laughed as we heard of the bossy exploits of the bossy teachers. There was one who even tried to boss the school hamster and was bitten on the finger when she shook it at him. Then there was one who always said exactly the same bossy things at exactly the same time of day. This bossy teacher found that

her class was able to predict what she was going to say and said it for her even before she opened her mouth. She had to make up a whole new list of things about which to boss people after that.

We stopped for the night and continued the task the following day. Then, just before midday, I opened the last letter and handed it to Aunt Harmonica. This last letter did not count at all, as it was from someone who went to a school where there was a bossy dog. This dog barked at you if you did anything which it thought was wrong, and thus was very unpopular. The only thing that the children at that school liked about the school dog was that when visiting sports teams came to the school, the school dog would rush out and nip the ankles of the visitors while the game was being played. This meant that the visitors always lost, which made the school dog into something of a hero.

"Now," said Aunt Harmonica, sounding very relieved, "let's look at the third pile."

There were only three letters in the third

pile and my aunts looked at them very carefully. They read them and then re-read them. Then they held them up to the light in the hope that that would help. At last, after much discussion between themselves, they chose one.

"This girl must be talking about Majolica," said Aunt Veronica. "Look, she says here that this teacher goes red in the face when she starts to boss people around."

"That's exactly what Majolica used to do," agreed Aunt Harmonica. "And look, she says that they even found her being bossy when nobody was there to boss around."

"Majolica often used to do that," said Aunt Veronica. "Yes. There's no doubt about it. We've found our sister!"

We made a large bonfire of all the other letters and then prepared to leave the campsite. The letter had come from some distance away, and Aunt Veronica said that we would need quite some time for the journey. If we set off at once, we could find a place to stop overnight and would reach the school the next morning.

So we said good-bye to the farmer and thanked him for his kindness. Then we set off, the farmer standing on his doorstep looking very puzzled as to how the trailer made no noise when it moved. I waved to him from my window, and he waved back, but when I looked again he was scratching his head in utter bewilderment.

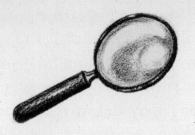

The Bossiest Teacher

We found the school with little difficulty. It was midmorning by the time we arrived and so the children were all in their classrooms having lessons. I wondered what we were going to do next, but Aunt Veronica soon answered that question.

"We'll stay right here," she said. "When the children come out at lunchtime, we'll see Majolica. I can guarantee that."

I wasn't sure what she meant, but I knew that things always seemed to work out with Aunt Veronica so I did not worry.

When we heard the lunch bell, Aunt Veronica got out of the trailer and stood at the school gates. The gates were made of iron bars and over the years had become a bit twisted. They looked as if one or two cars had backed into them at times, and there were also places where bars had slipped out of their places and had not been put back.

Rolling up her sleeves, Aunt Veronica took out one of the misshapen bars and began to twist it back into shape. Some of the children noticed this, and came running to watch her. Soon others saw what was going on, and joined them. Within minutes, there was a large crowd cheering with delight as Aunt Veronica bent the gate back into proper shape.

There was the sound of a shrill voice from the other side of the playground. Out of the main door of the school, a large figure advanced purposefully.

"What are you doing, children?" the voice screeched. "Have you nothing better to do than hang around the gates? What about your lunch? How do you expect to grow properly if you don't eat lunch? Well, come on, answer me!"

The figure paused, noticing what was attracting the children.

"And you!" the teacher shouted at Aunt Veronica. "Put the school gates down immediately! We simply won't have people twisting the school gates like that! Did you hear me? Put those gates down at once! This instant!"

Aunt Veronica ignored the order and continued to twist the gates. She had almost finished, and the gates were beginning to look straight again.

"Did you not hear me?" barked the teacher, advancing toward Aunt Veronica. "Do I have to repeat everything several times? Is there something wrong with your ears, may I ask?"

Aunt Veronica gave a last great twist on the iron bars and then looked up. When the teacher saw her, she stopped in her tracks.

"Veronica!" she exclaimed.

Aunt Veronica's face burst into a smile. "Majolica!"

Then Aunt Veronica rushed forward to hug her sister.

"She's going to twist the teacher!" cried somebody in alarm. But when they saw the smile of delight on Aunt Majolica's face, they knew that everything was all right.

I was a little bit frightened of Aunt Majolica to begin with, but after a few minutes I realized that underneath the bossiness she was really very kind. As we sat in the trailer and talked, she asked all about my father and myself and told me how happy she was that we had found her.

"Now there's something we must ask you," said Aunt Veronica when there was a short break in the conversation. "Do you, by any chance, know what happened to Thessalonika and Japonica?"

I waited with bated breath for an answer. I was prepared for a disappointment and for Aunt Majolica to deny all knowledge of them, but she said something quite different.

"Of course," she said. "I see them for tea every Sunday at three o'clock."

Aunt Veronica and Aunt Harmonica

clapped their hands together with pleasure and I let out a whoop of delight.

"Then we can get in touch with them?" I said. "Can we call them this afternoon?"

Aunt Majolica looked at me in surprise.

"Oh no," she said. "That won't be necessary. Anyway, I don't think they have a telephone in their house. Or at least, they've never mentioned one to me."

"In that case," said Aunt Veronica, "can we go and see them?"

"That won't be necessary either," said Aunt Majolica. "They'll know to come."

We all looked very puzzled.

"I don't understand," said Aunt Harmonica eventually. "How will they know that we want to see them?"

As she spoke the question, I began to realize what Aunt Majolica meant. My father had said that the twins had an extraordinary ability to read minds. Did this mean that they would know what we were thinking, even if they weren't here?

Aunt Majolica answered my question before I even asked it.

"All I have to do is think really hard," she explained. "If I stand still and think: 'Thessalonika! Japonica! Please come and see me!' they'll come. You watch."

While Aunt Majolica and Aunt Harmonica sat in the trailer and waited for the arrival of the last two aunts, Aunt Veronica and I went into the playground to find the girl who had sent in the winning letter. The advertisement had promised a prize for the winner, and we had not forgotten the promise.

"But what are we going to give her?" I asked Aunt Veronica. "We haven't bought her anything."

Aunt Veronica turned and whispered, "There are some things that can't be bought. These things are by far the most valuable."

I wasn't sure what she meant by this, but I didn't have time to find out, as the girl whose name we had asked had been pointed out to us, and Aunt Veronica was making her way toward her.

The girl was very pleased to hear that she had been successful.

"We like our teacher," she said. "We really do. But she is very bossy!"

Aunt Veronica nodded. "She's always been like that," she said. "Right from the time she learned to talk. Her first words were bossy ones. Can you believe that?" The girl laughed.

"Now," Aunt Veronica continued, "I promised you a prize, and a prize you will get. I'm not going to give you anything you can touch, or keep, or eat. I'm going to show you something that you'll be able to use for the rest of your life. It will need a little bit of work on your part before you can do it properly, but if you do the exercises as I tell you, I promise that you'll be able to do it."

The girl's eyes lit up with excitement.

"I'll do them!" she said enthusiastically.

"Good," said Aunt Veronica. "Now listen to me. Do you like to eat nuts?"

"I do," said the girl. "I love them."

"Very well," said Aunt Veronica. "And

when you have a nut, can you usually find the nutcrackers?"

The girl shook her head. "Never," she said.

"So I imagine that you would like to be able to crack nuts with your fingers?"

"I'd love that," said the girl. "But it's impossible. Nuts are far too hard for that."

"You're wrong," said Aunt Veronica. "Look."

Aunt Veronica reached into a pocket and took out a large walnut. Holding it between her thumb and forefinger, she gave it a quick flip and cracked it neatly into four pieces.

The girl was very impressed, and she watched closely as Aunt Veronica showed her how to do it.

"As I told you," she said, "you'll have to practice. But all you do is move this finger like this . . . and then this finger a little like that . . . and then you push down there, and turn the thumb around through there and . . ." *Crunch!* Another walnut had been cracked. The girl watched carefully and then

Aunt Veronica gave her a few walnuts to use for practice. Then, thanking her again for helping us find Aunt Majolica, we returned to the trailer.

I opened the door and went in. There, sitting on a stool was a tall, rather thin lady. She looked at me carefully through the tiny pair of glasses that perched on the end of her nose, and I knew at once that I had found another aunt. It was Thessalonika or Japonica, but I had no idea which one.

To the Detectives' office

"Thessalonika," said the new aunt, "I could tell that you were uncertain which one I was."

I went forward and shook hands with Aunt Thessalonika. She had a kind face, and I knew at once that I was going to like her. The only problem, of course, was her mind reading. Could she really tell what people were thinking? And if she could, then I'd have to be very careful not to think about anything rude.

That's very difficult, you know. Just you try it. Imagine that somebody else, maybe your best friend, could tell what was in your mind, and imagine that you knew it. The very first thing you'll think about is something that you wouldn't want her to know you were thinking about, and this happens even if you weren't thinking about it before.

"Don't worry," said Aunt Thessalonika, as if she knew exactly what was on my mind. "I don't read minds all the time. I find it a bit exhausting, you see, so I only use my powers at work."

"Your aunt Thessalonika is a detective," explained Aunt Majolica. "She and your aunt Japonica have a detective agency."

"That's right," said Aunt Thessalonika. "And that's why Aunt Japonica isn't here at the moment. We're in the middle of a very important investigation and I shall have to return to it in a very short time. In fact, I can tell that Japonica is becoming a bit annoyed, and so I'd better leave right now."

She rose to her feet.

"There's a good place to park your trailer in our backyard," she explained. "Majolica will show you the way. We can all meet back there this evening."

"May I come with you?" I asked, not wanting to lose my new aunt so soon after finding her.

Aunt Thessalonika looked at me and frowned.

"We have an awful lot of confidential matters in our office," she said. "Can you keep a secret?"

"Of course," I assured her.

She looked at Aunt Veronica, who nodded encouragingly.

"In that case," she said, "you may come."

The door of my aunts' office had a bell and a small peephole. Aunt Thessalonika ushered me inside and led me along a narrow corridor to a further door at the end. This door was locked, and she fiddled with several keys for a moment or two before it opened.

Inside, I found myself in a large room with no windows at all, but it had a high skylight that let in the daylight. The room was lined with shelves and cupboards, and at the far end there were two desks. A tall man was sitting at one of the desks, and he looked up sharply when we came in. Aunt Thessalonika jerked her head in the direction of this man and told me to go and say hello to him.

"How do you do?" said the man, rising to his feet as I approached his desk. "So you're Harriet."

I was astonished to hear that he knew my name, and I assumed that Aunt Thessalonika must have called to say that we were coming.

We shook hands and he asked me to sit down. I did so and studied the man before me. He had a large mustache, gray hair, and a pair of heavy glasses. He was the sort of man you could walk past in the street without ever noticing. Looking at his mustache, which was rather bushy, I wondered how he cut it. Did he use . . .

"Scissors," said the man. "Most people with mustaches use scissors."

I gasped. Here was another mind reader!

Were all private detectives mind readers, or was it just my two aunts and their friends?

"However," the man went on, rising to his feet, "this mustache never needs to be cut at all. And why is that?" He paused, his eyes glinting through the thick lenses of his heavy glasses. "It's because it is utterly and completely . . . false!"

And with that he ripped the mustache off his face with a quick flick of his wrist.

"Nor," he continued, "do I have to spend too much time combing this hair, because it, you see, is . . . a wig!"

And with another flourish he ripped off the wig and I saw his real hair tumble out from beneath. And then I realized—he was a woman. In fact, he was my aunt. It was Aunt Japonica in disguise.

As I stared in astonishment, Aunt Japonica took off the rest of her disguise with a few deft movements. Off came the suit, to reveal a shiny green dress underneath. Off came the glasses and, with a wipe of a handkerchief, off came the makeup.

"Now you see me as I really am," said Aunt Japonica with a sigh. "But I love disguises, and I'm so glad that our job requires us to dress up so much."

"She's very good at it," chipped in Aunt Thessalonika. "You should see her disguised as a nun."

"Or as a bus driver," added Aunt Japonica.

"And what about the time you were a dog?" said Aunt Thessalonika. "Tell her about that."

"Oh yes!" said Aunt Japonica, her face creased with pleasure. "That was a case where we had to try and trap somebody in a park. I managed to get hold of a dog's outfit and I dressed up in it. Everybody thought I was a large dog, even the other dogs."

"Yes," said Aunt Thessalonika, "and everything would have gone very well if the dogcatcher hadn't come and spoiled it all."

"I'll never forgive him," said Aunt Japonica. "I felt so ashamed being dragged away like that in his awful dogcatcher's van. But I got my own back in the end."

"How did you do that?" I asked.

"I asked him the time when he opened the back of the van to get me out at the other end," said Aunt Japonica, with a smile. "He got such a fright that he dropped his keys and ran. I drove his van back to the park, but by that time the person we were planning to trap had gone. It was a great shame."

After Aunt Japonica had finished her story, I glanced at the room around me. It was full of very intriguing things, and I was on the point of asking to be shown around when Aunt Thessalonika suggested that we do just that.

"I can tell you'd like to see some of our things," she said, mind reading again. "Is that all right with you, Japonica?"

"Of course," said Aunt Japonica. "Let's start with some of the disguises."

I was led by Aunt Japonica to a large cupboard in a corner. She opened the doors with pride and I saw inside an array of extraordinary outfits. There was a uniform of the French Foreign Legion; there was the outfit of a Russian sailor. Then there was a doctor's white coat and a ballet dancer's tutu. There were many others.

Next, Aunt Japonica opened a drawer to the side of the cupboard. Inside were all sorts of devices to stick on your face. There were scars—straight and curved—there were pimples and spots (these were for use if you wanted to look like a teenager). Then there were false ears and false noses—all very realistic—and several kinds of false chins.

"I could make you look like anyone," Aunt Japonica said proudly. "I could pass you off as the president of the United States himself, if I wanted to."

"That's enough of that," said Aunt Thessalonika rather impatiently. "There are other things in the office, you know."

I followed Aunt Thessalonika past a row of neatly stacked notebooks.

"Our old cases," she said proudly. "We keep notes on everything we do."

I stopped and looked at some of the titles. "The Case of the Double-cracked Mirror." "The Case of the Vanishing Bus." "The Case of the Poisonous Lettuce." ("A very disturbing case," said Aunt Thessalonika, shaking her head rather grimly.)

Next we came to a shelf that was full of magnifying glasses. I was wondering why the aunts needed so many of them, when Aunt Thessalonika took one of them off the shelf and showed it to me.

"These are no ordinary magnifying glasses," she said, her voice lowered almost to a whisper. "Look through that."

I held the glass over a section of the shelf and stared through it. All I saw were fingerprints.

"You see," said Aunt Thessalonika, "that's our fingerprint glass. If you look at anything with that magnifying glass, you'll see any fingerprints that happen to be around. It's a very great help, I can assure you."

I picked up another magnifying glass and showed it to Aunt Thessalonika.

"What does this one do?" I asked.

Aunt Thessalonika took it from me and examined it for a moment.

"Ah!" she said. "That one's very useful indeed. There aren't many of these around."

"But what does it do?" I pressed.

"Translates French into English," said Aunt Thessalonika. "Look."

She reached for a book off another shelf and opened it. I could see that the book was written in French.

"Now look at this page through the magnifying glass," said Aunt Thessalonika.

I held the glass over the page and looked through it. At first the words seemed a little bit blurred, but when I moved the magnifying glass slightly they became clearer. What is more, they were in English!

"This one does German," said Aunt Thessalonika, pointing to another, very heavy and serious-looking magnifying glass. "And this one," she went on, pointing to a very elegant magnifying glass with swirls of silver around the handle, "does Italian."

We moved around the room, examining all the bits and pieces that my aunts used in their unusual work. There were bags of coins, all neatly labeled; there were maps; there were pens that wrote in different colors. At one point I picked up a large white object and asked Aunt Thessalonika what it was. "That," she said, "is very strange. It still puzzles us."

"Yes," agreed Aunt Japonica. "We haven't heard the last of that."

Aunt Thessalonika took the object from me and placed it under a light.

"This is a plaster cast," she said. "I take it that you know what a plaster cast is?"

I nodded. I had made casts at school, pouring the plaster into shapes to make impressions.

"Well," continued Aunt Thessalonika, "you'll see that this plaster cast is of a footprint."

I felt rather disappointed by this news. I was hoping that it would be something much more exciting than that.

"Look at the toes," said Aunt Thessalonika grimly. "Count them."

I counted out the number of dents in the plaster where the toes had been. Six!

"Precisely!" said Aunt Japonica. "Six. What do you make of that?"

"I don't know," I replied truthfully.

"Neither do we," said Aunt Thessalonika. "But we will certainly make it our business to find out!"

Suddenly Aunt Japonica looked at her watch.

"My goodness," she said. "Time is flying past. We have work to do, I'm afraid. You can sit in that chair over there and read a book until it's time for us to go to join the others."

So I sat in the chair and read. Or rather, I tried to read, but my concentration kept slipping, and I sneaked glances at what my two aunts were doing. They were fussing over their desks, fiddling with microscopes and magnifying glasses, and whispering to one another. I tried hard to hear what they were saying, but it was impossible. So I gave up in the end and just waited until they were ready to go.

At last they packed up their work, locked the office behind them, and drove me off to their house. There in the backyard was the trailer, with the table set with tea, sandwiches, and cakes, and Majolica bossing all the others around, getting things ready on time. I felt tremendously proud of myself. It had taken a little time, but at last I had assembled all my aunts in one place.

There was only one thing left to do. Now that I had found my five aunts, it was time to take them all back to show my father. Then, if only I managed to find a painter, we could have the painting finished. Not only that, of course, but the family that had been so unhappily split up so many years ago would be together again.

We traveled back that day. It was very hard work for Aunt Veronica, pedaling the trailer with all those aunts in the back, but she managed. Every few miles I would pass her a chocolate bar, which she would swallow almost in one gulp. This seemed to keep her strength up.

At last we drew up to our house. I left the

aunts in the trailer while I went in the front door. There was my father, sitting in his usual chair with his slippers on, doing a crossword puzzle.

"Hello," he said. "I see you're back."

"I am," I replied.

"Did you have a good time?" he asked, hardly raising his eyes from the puzzle.

"Yes," I said. It was clear to me that he had forgotten all about my search for the aunts, so I slipped outside and signaled for the aunts to come in.

My father looked up from his puzzle and turned quite pale. For a moment I thought he was going to faint, but then, with a sound somewhere between a groan and a gasp, he rose to his feet.

"Harold!" said Aunt Majolica. "Look at the state of your slippers! When did you clean them last?"

Before my father had the opportunity to answer, all five aunts dashed across the room to give him a hug. Unfortunately, they knocked him back into his chair, and Aunts

Thessalonika and Japonica ended up sprawled all over him.

When they untangled each other, the aunts all stood around him, kissing him on the cheek and patting his shoulders. They were talking so much that nobody could hear what anybody else was saying. My father, however, seemed to be happy to see all his sisters, so I left them together and went up to my room.

I had left the painting behind my wardrobe, safely covered with an old sheet. Now I took it out and carried it downstairs, still draped in its sheet. My aunts were all so busy talking when I entered the room that at first nobody paid much attention to me. Then, one by one, they began to notice the large covered object that I was holding, and they fell silent.

"What on earth is that?" asked Aunt Majolica.

"It's something I very much want to show you all," I began. "In fact, it's the reason why I started to look for you in the first place."

"What can she mean?" asked Aunt Veronica, looking puzzled.

"I have no idea," replied Aunt Japonica, who was too tired and too excited to do any mind reading.

I waited until they were silent again and then, with a dramatic pull at the sheet, I exposed the painting. As the picture came into view, there were gasps from several of the aunts.

"Oh my goodness!" exclaimed Aunt Thessalonika. "It's that picture . . . the one that was never finished." Aunt Majolica took several steps forward and examined the painting more closely.

"I believe you're right," she said. "Yes, look at the barn! And look, I'm wearing my favorite bracelet—the one I got for my tenth birthday."

The other aunts crowded around to examine the picture and all of them seemed quite delighted.

"I never thought I'd see it again," said Aunt Majolica, reaching for a handkerchief she had tucked into her sleeve. "Oh dear! This is just all too much for me."

And at that, she burst into tears of emotion, closely followed by her sisters. I let them weep for a moment, and then I made my announcement.

"I think we should have this picture completed," I said. "We can find the painter, or if we can't find him, we can find another. Then we'll at last have the family portrait that grandfather and grandmother always wanted."

The aunts were silent for a moment as they considered my suggestion. Then, almost with one voice, they shouted their agreement.

"A brilliant idea!" crooned Aunt Veronica. "Let's contact the painter this very moment!"

Of course, it was not quite that easy. Although Aunt Japonica remembered the painter's name, he had long since left the house he was living in at the time when he had started the picture. Aunt Japonica and Aunt Thessalonika, however, pointed out that if anybody could find him it would be them, and that the rest of us should give them two hours to do so. So they dashed off and only an hour and a half later they came back, looking flushed with excitement.

"We've found him," they announced proudly. "It wasn't easy, but we found him." They paused before continuing, "And what's more, he has agreed to come to finish the painting first thing tomorrow morning."

There was general jubilation at this news, and the aunts all began to talk again. I left the room, leaving the painting propped against a wall. I was delighted to have found all my aunts, but I felt that it would be best to leave them to themselves for a little while.

I could hardly wait, though, for the picture to be finished. I could already imagine it above the fireplace in our living room. I would show all my friends and announce: "My aunts!" Nobody would have as many aunts as that and I knew that everybody was bound to be very impressed. I must admit that this thought rather pleased me.

The aunts talked late into the night, until well after I had gone to bed. Then, taking themselves off to the sofas and piles of cushions, which they had set up in various odd corners of the house, they went to bed. In the silence of the darkened house, Aunt Harmonica threw her voice once or twice, but she was told by Aunt Majolica that everybody wanted to get to sleep. So she stopped, and the quiet returned.

The Finished Painting

The painter arrived early the next morning, exactly as promised. He was just as I had imagined him, although his mustache now drooped a little at the edges. When he saw the painting, his eyes lit up and he clapped his hands together.

"So there it is at last!" he exclaimed. "And it's exactly as I remember it. I've always wanted to finish it, and now I have the chance."

Without further ado, he hoisted the painting onto an easel and opened his large case of paints. Then, when he had struggled into a billowing white painting smock, which made him look just a little like a blimp, he arranged my father and all the aunts into two rows.

"Don't move," he said. "It's very important that you keep absolutely still."

I watched as he began to paint. His brush moved quickly, and every now and then he leaned forward and peered at one of the aunts.

"I hope that he doesn't make my nose look too big," I heard Aunt Majolica whisper to Aunt Japonica.

"And I shall be very disappointed if he notices that my left ear is bigger than my right," whispered back Aunt Japonica.

The painter painted for several hours. By the end of that time, I could see that my father and the aunts were beginning to feel tired of standing still, and they were relieved when the painter told them that they could have a break. They went off to sit down, but a few minutes later he had them all back again, and he painted for the rest of that day without stopping.

At the end of the day, he stood back, inspected the painting, and then closed his paint case with a snap.

"It's finished," he said. "That's it."

This announcement caused a buzz of excitement among the aunts.

"I can't wait to see it," announced Aunt Veronica.

The painter shook his head.

"I'm afraid you'll have to wait," he said. "I don't want anybody to see it until the last of the paint is dry." He looked at his watch. "And that should be at about three o'clock tomorrow afternoon."

"Then we will have an unveiling ceremony," Aunt Majolica said. "We'll all gather in the living room and the picture can be officially unveiled by . . ."

She looked around. Every one of the other aunts was looking expectant, hoping that she would be chosen for this important task.

"By Harriet!" concluded Aunt Majolica.

I was very excited to have been chosen to unveil the picture, and every minute between then and three o'clock the next afternoon seemed to drag interminably.

When the time for the ceremony came at last, we all gathered in the living room. The painter had arrived as well, and he had moved the painting, still covered, into a prominent place in front of the fireplace. The aunts had been busy in the kitchen the previous evening, and the tables were laden with cakes and sandwiches. Even my father, who had looked rather strained since all his sisters had arrived, was smiling and rubbing his hands with pleasure at the thought of seeing the finished picture at last.

When everything was prepared, I was ushered up to the front of the picture. The painter stood beside me, and when everybody was silent he nodded in my direction. My heart thumping with excitement, I reached out and took the edge of the cloth in my right hand. Then, with a firm tug, I pulled, and the cloth fell away to reveal the finished picture below.

Nobody said a word. My father and all the

aunts peered at the picture, their eyes narrowed, their mouths open, as they took in the details. Then, with a wail, Aunt Majolica broke the silence.

"Oh no!" she wailed. "You've . . . You've put the heads on the wrong bodies!"

What followed was very upsetting. The aunts all crowded around the painting and looked at it more closely. When they were satisfied that a mistake had indeed been made, they turned on the painter and began to scold him severely.

"You've painted Thessalonika's head on my shoulders!" protested Aunt Japonica. "Look. That's definitely my body and that's undoubtedly her head!"

The painter's jaw dropped and his mustache seemed to wiggle like the tail of a rabbit caught in a trap. There was really very little he could say to excuse himself, and he just had to stand there and accept his scolding.

"Well!" said Aunt Majolica at the end of it all. "That's that, then. The painting is ruined. I will never be able to look at it again."

"Nor will I," agreed Aunt Veronica. "It's totally spoiled."

The painter, still looking very miserable, at last was able to summon up the courage to say something.

"Please forgive me," he began. "I understand how you must feel. But I think I may be able to do something about it."

"And what would that be?" demanded Aunt Majolica in her bossiest voice. "I don't see how you can fix it now. You can't rub out oil paint, you know."

The painter held up his hand. "Please just give me two hours," he said. "That's all it will take."

Still grumbling, the aunts agreed that he could take the painting into the kitchen and do whatever he had to do with it. None of them thought that he would be able to do much, though, and they continued to complain among themselves well after he had left the room. I felt sorry for the painter. I had often enough made mistakes with pictures to know just how upsetting it is to work for hours on something and then realize that your efforts were to no avail.

Barely two hours later, the painter returned. He had covered the painting in a cloth again, but this time he didn't dare say that everybody should wait until the paint was dry before they saw it. He beckoned to me and told me that I should unveil it again. So once again I stood beside the painting and gave the cloth a tug.

As the cloth fell away there was a gasp from all the aunts. Then, after a dreadful moment of suspense, Aunt Majolica gave a cheer.

"Brilliant!" she said. "What a brilliant idea!"

"I agree," called out Aunt Thessalonika. "Really, that was the only thing to do."

I looked at the painting and caught my breath. The bodies of my father and the aunts had all disappeared—painted over with blue waves of the sea. Only their heads showed now, bobbing above the waves. And of course

this meant that nobody could tell that the heads were on the wrong bodies, as everything below was covered with thick blue paint. And the barn, which had been the background, was now a ship.

Everybody was pleased. The cakes, which had not been touched since the terrible mistake had been discovered, were now passed around, as were the sandwiches and the glasses of homemade lemonade. The painter, relieved at having solved the problem so neatly, beamed with pleasure, and his mustache was soon covered with cream and icing. I was happy to see all my aunts so happy and was also proud that what my poor grandparents had wanted so long ago was now done.

That evening, after the painter had gone home, we continued with the party. Aunt Harmonica, who was a very good cook, prepared a special meal, and we sat at the table with paper hats on, just as if it were Christmas.

"It's been so very, very long," said Aunt Veronica. "We must never allow ourselves to drift apart again."

"We will visit you every week," said Aunt Japonica.

"Without fail," chimed in Aunt Thessalonika.

"Oh, the fun we'll have!" added Aunt Majolica.

I said very little. They were so busy talking about the old days and what they had done as children that nobody had much time to listen to me. But that didn't matter. What was important to me was that I had found my aunts and had made my grandparents' wish come true.

And what amazing aunts they were! I could see that we were going to have extraordinary adventures together, and in fact that is just what happened. Perhaps I will be able to tell you about some of those adventures one day. And I will also tell you about the trick my father played on Aunt Majolica. I don't have time to do that now. But I *can* tell you that it was very funny—very funny indeed . . .

Don't miss any adventure, mystery, and fun with these Alexander McCall Smith titles!

 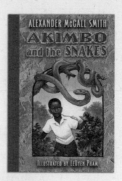

Now available in paperback!

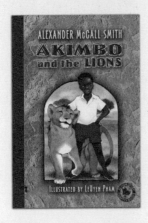

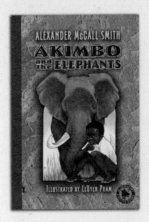

A Note on the Author

Graham Clark

ALEXANDER MCCALL SMITH has written more than fifty books, including the *New York Times* bestselling No. 1 Ladies' Detective Agency mysteries and The Sunday Philosophy Club series. A professor of medical law at Edinburgh University, he was born in what is now Zimbabwe and taught law at the University of Botswana. He lives in Edinburgh, Scotland.

Visit him at WWW.ALEXANDERMCCALLSMITH.COM

A Note on the Illustrator

LAURA RANKIN is also the illustrator of the picture books *Rabbit Ears*, *Swan Harbor*, and *The Handmade Alphabet*. She lives in Maine.

John Stephenson